MW00902421

Maggie
the
Monkey Photographer

Written by: Shauna Usher
Illustrated by: Emily Matthews

WRITERS REPUBLIC L.L.C.
515 Summit Ave. Unit R1
Union City, NJ 07087, USA

Website: *www.writersrepublic.com*
Hotline: *1-877-656-6838*
Email: *info@writersrepublic.com*

Ordering Information:
Quantity sales. Special discounts are available on quantity purchases by corporations, associations, and others. For details, contact the publisher at the address above.

Library of Congress Control Number: 2021936881
ISBN-13:   978-1-63728-053-9   [Paperback Edition]
                  978-1-63728-457-5   [Hardback Edition]
                  978-1-63728-054-6   [Digital Edition]

Rev. date: 04/09/2021

To my best friend, thank you for always believing in me and encouraging me to never give up on my dreams.

Maggie the monkey loved taking pictures. She searched high up in the trees and low down in the swamps.

She walked through the fields full of flowers, and she hiked high up in the snowy mountains. She wanted to get the perfect picture.

Maggie loved taking pictures so much, she decided to open,

Maggie's Photography.

Maggie went bananas getting her business ready. She was so excited that she ran to tell her family and friends.

When she told her family, her parents were worried, her brother said it was silly, and her sister threw her head back and laughed.

Maggie was so upset. "Nobody believes in me", she thought. She climbed high up in a tall tree, to sit in silence.

Maggie heard laughing down by the creek. She poked her head out from the top of the branches to see Gracie the gator, taking pictures of her friends.

Maggie was so sad. "I'll never be as good as Gracie the gator." She strolled down the path to Tiny the turtle's house.

"Hi, Maggie!" said Tiny.

"Hi, Tiny." said Maggie.

Tiny noticed Maggie wasn't her cheerful self.

"What's wrong?" Tiny asked.

"I really like taking pictures but I'm not any good at it." said Maggie.

Tiny was shocked to hear his friend talk like this. He looked up at her and said, "Maggie, you have a huge imagination and see the world in a special way. You show it through your pictures, and I love seeing the pictures you take."

This made Maggie smile.

"Thanks Tiny. You always know how to make me feel better." said Maggie.

"You're welcome. Now, go take pictures." said Tiny.

Maggie went on her way down the path, taking pictures as she went.

While on the path, she walked pass Lily the ladybug, who was relaxing on a beautiful sunflower.

"Hi Lily." said Maggie.

"Hi Maggie." said Lily.

"Can I take your picture?" asked Maggie.

"Sure!" said Lily, excited that Maggie wanted to take her picture.

Down the path Maggie went, whistling as she skipped. Maggie stopped when she heard a familiar tune. It was Perry the parrot, whistling his favorite pirate song.

"Hi, Perry!" said Maggie.

"Hi, Maggie." whistled Perry.

"Can I take your picture?" asked Maggie.

"Absolutely." squawked Perry, happy to help his friend.

Maggie took the picture and showed Perry.

"You sure arrrre good" said Perry.

"Thanks Perry." said Maggie.

Maggie skipped down the path, smiling from ear to ear. She saw Ellie the elephant, Sally the sloth, and Froogie the frog playing jump rope.

"Hey Maggie!" shouted Ellie the elephant. Maggie walked over.

"Maggie will you take our picture?" asked Sally the sloth.

"How did you know I take pictures?" Maggie asked.

"Gracie the gator told us," said Froogie the frog. "She said you are really good."

Maggie was shocked, "Gracie thinks I'm a good photographer?" she thought. Maggie took their picture and showed them before she went on her way.

Maggie climbed up to her house. "Hi, Momma." she said. "Hi, Maggie. What did you do today?" Momma asked. "I took pictures. Would you like to see them?" Momma nodded her head yes and walked to Maggie.

Momma was surprised at how good the pictures were. Papa and Maggie's brother and sister came to see the pictures too. They all loved them and told Maggie how wonderful her pictures were.

Maggie's family loved her pictures so much they decided to help her with Maggie's Photography. Maggie was so happy she ran to Tiny's house to tell him the good news.

"Thank you Tiny for believing in me."

said Maggie. "You're welcome Maggie. I knew you could do it. Just always remember and never forget; you can do anything you put your mind to. Everyone is special in their own way."

The End